# The Great Tree

A CHRISTMAS FABLE

Written by: Able Barrett

The Last Road Dog Publications
14308 S. Goss Rd., Cheney, WA 99004

Able Barrett/The Last Road Dog Publications
14308 S. Goss Rd
Cheney, WA 99004
www.thelastroaddog.com

Publisher's Note: This is a work of fiction. Names, characters, places, and incidents are a product of the author's imagination. Locales and public names are sometimes used for atmospheric purposes. Any resemblance to actual people, living or dead, or to businesses, companies, events, institutions, or locales is completely coincidental.

Book Layout © 2021 BookDesignTemplates.com

The Great Tree/ Able Barrett. – 2nd ed.
ISBN 9781667864631

In Loving Memory of Demerri
My Dear Departed Rescued Dog
The Best German Shepard I Ever Knew & Loved
All profits from the sale of this book go to
<u>The Last Road Dog Animal Sanctuary</u>
for the rescue of dogs, cats, and horses

# CHAPTER ONE

# A Christmas Past

Children often stared with great awe at the huge evergreen tree that stood upon the distant mountain stretched against the broad horizon. The tree's enormous size made it appear closer than it actually was. None of the children, however, had actually seen the tree up close; not from the want of many a brave warrior child who had attempted the quest only to be foiled. Stories had been told for generations about missing children. No one knew truth from fantasy. All that the children were told was that any child that entered the forest leading up to the Great Tree and the Castle disappeared, and they were neither seen nor heard from again. All the town's folks, young and old alike, had grown up with fables told by fireplaces, late at night when the moon was full, and wolves sang their endless serenades in the pale glow of the moonlight. It was foretold in these fables that wolves were the vanguard of the evil Sorcerer's kingdom and stalked the territory in search of invaders to the province. These wolves had the strength of bulls and the speed and swiftness of gazelles, with eyes that glowed with rings of fire that streaked as they crisscrossed the land. Their numbers were few and they were led by the Great Black Wolf and the Charnelgoul.

The Great Tree stood next to a castle. The enormity of the Great Tree made the castle appear dwarfed in stature, and this made the attraction of the Great Tree even more magnetic. Christmas was falling upon the land once more.

# CHAPTER TWO

# A Boy & His Dog

The town's main street was lined with little shops furnishing their wares for the townspeople and the occasional traveler that passed through the remote village to buy. On the third day before Christmas, one such traveler ventured into town. At his side was a handsome large white dog. The young traveler had rescued her many years before from a hard driving dog sled musher in the vast nomadic territory in the uncharted lands east of the majestic mountain range. The musher had treated her terribly and abused her with a club. The young man challenged the musher's mistreatment of the dog and defeated the musher in a game of chance and skill, winning her freedom. Although freedom was hers, she thereafter never left the young man's side. She was thought to be part wolf and part German Shepherd.

The traveler was a very handsome young boy with dark hair. As the traveler and his dog made their way down the main street, two children ran up to see the big dog that was approaching.

"What a great dog!" said the young boy.

"Wow! What's his name?" asked the young girl who was with the boy.

"Her name is Jenny. What are your names?"

"My name is Michael, and this is my sister Madeline," said the boy, gesturing toward Madeline.

"Hello, nice to meet you both. I'm Andrew. How old are you kids?"

"I am seven, and my sister is nine," replied Michael.

"Where are you from?" asked Madeline.

"I'm from a land far, far away from here."

"Why are you here?" asked Madeline.

"I have come to see the owner of the castle that sits upon the mountain."

"No! No!" the kids replied in unison. "You can't go up there. No one who goes there ever comes back." Michael and Madeline retold the fables of the Great Tree, the evil Sorcerer, the Great Black Wolf, the Charnelgoul, and the missing children.

Andrew assured the kids that he would be safe. He told them that he had "magical powers" that would protect him. Although Andrew did not possess any magical powers, he felt it would push any imaginary fears that his two new friends might have out of their young minds. He asked them if the Great Tree had an inn where he could spend the night. Michael told him that their older sister ran the inn on the other side of the village and eagerly said, "Come on, we'll show you the way."

As they walked to the inn, the kids continued to ask him all sorts of questions about his upcoming journey to the castle. They finally reached the inn, and the children quickly ran in, yelling for their older sister. As Andrew entered the inn, a young lady greeted him.

"Hi, I'm Aurora. I am the innkeeper here."

The children were excitedly telling Aurora about Andrew's upcoming ascent to the castle and the Great Tree.

"Please, kids, let the young man alone. Go play outside while I take care of getting our guest a room," said Aurora as she waved the children outside. The children quickly ran out of the inn to spread the news of the stranger's assault on the castle.

"Sorry about those two. They are a handful. I am their older sister. Our mom and dad died of the fever last year, so I am taking care of them and trying to run this inn as well."

"I am sorry, Aurora."

After a pause, Andrew continued, "Wow, that is a lot of responsibility. I am impressed."

"You do what you have to do to get along."

"They seem like great kids."

"Thank you, but it is just luck. It is pretty common these days for us to have to take care of things after our parents die."

"That's true. My father died in a mountaineering expedition, and my mother is sick with the fever as well. So I understand."

"I am sorry about your parents."

"Thanks . . . Hey, you mind if my dog, Jenny, stays with me in the room? She is quite well-behaved, and she will be of no trouble to you."

"That's fine. She's quite beautiful."

"Thank you."

Aurora showed Andrew his room.

"Thank you, Aurora."

"Sure. If you need anything, just let me know. Good

night, you two."

"Good night."

The room at the inn had a window that faced the Great Tree with the castle by its side. As Andrew gazed through the window at the castle, his mind wandered back to his mother, who was at home sick with the deadly fever. Although she wanted to see her lost son one more time before she passed, she insisted that Andrew not look for him, for it was much too dangerous. She made Andrew promise that he would not venture off and search for his brother. Andrew agreed not to. Andrew was now looking for his brother, Nicholas, in defiance of his mother's wishes. He had made up his mind that he could not live with himself if he did not try. He understood his mother's concern, but he felt he had to do what he thought was right. He lied to his mother out of love for her and because he did not want her worrying about him on his quest. Right or wrong, it was the way he felt about it. Nicholas had been abducted by an evil Sorcerer, an evil wizard of sorts, when they were both very young. Nicholas was his older brother. Andrew had been searching for Nicholas for weeks; he was now at a small mountain village where he had hoped to find Nicholas and bring him back to his mother before she died. With Jenny at his side, Andrew, weary from his lengthy travels, fell soundly asleep while gazing at the castle in the distance.

## CHAPTER THREE

# The Journey

The next morning Andrew awoke to the sound of loud voices coming from a small crowd that had gathered in the lobby of the inn as he prepared his things for the ascent to the castle. As he and Jenny came down the stairs to the lobby, the noise became clearer. A crowd had gathered to see the man who was going to ascend to the castle in defiance of the evil Sorcerer. As they came into sight, the crowd became silent and just stared as the stranger and his dog made their way to the front desk. Aurora apologized for all the people, but they had heard the news of his planned trip to the castle.

"Don't be bothered, it's quite all right. I am just sorry that I caused such a stir in the town."

"Be careful, the journey you plan is known to be treacherous." Aurora seemed worried for Andrew.

"Yes, of course. I'll be careful. Promise. Well, then let's be off, shall we, Jen?" They proceeded through the crowd to the door of the inn. At the door, Andrew turned around and said, "Aurora, I'll see you again soon."

Out on the street, they began their journey to the castle. Madeline and Michael were waiting down the street, insisting on traveling with them on their trip to the castle. Andrew kept repeating "No!" but they were persistent. Finally, when they reached the very edge of the village, Andrew turned to them and told them if they followed him any further, he would put a deadly spell on them. They stopped and stared into Andrew's eyes, and he thought they believed him. They stood and watched until Andrew and Jenny vanished from sight, heading toward the castle. It had begun to snow. It was the second day before Christmas.

The journey was long. As Andrew and Jenny ascended the steep mountain path toward the castle, he remembered what his mother had told him. Andrew and his older brother, Nicholas, were much younger then. They were standing with their mother and father in the village near where they lived. It was late in the afternoon, and the stores were closing. They had all heard the stories of the evil Sorcerer and his rampages throughout the land, but they had never seen or even met anyone who had seen him, the evil Sorcerer. Suddenly the sun was eclipsed by the clouds. Lightning ignited in the sky, and a booming thunder roared through the village, a preluding march of the coming darkness. The wind rose and gales swept through the village, propelling dust, further masking the light of day. Andrew was standing next to Nicholas who was holding the hand of his little brother and trying to protect him from the sudden change in weather. Their parents had found an open store and called for their two boys to come in out of the street. It was too late; the evil Sorcerer swept down and grabbed both Nicholas and Andrew by their coats. Andrew was able to quickly wiggle his way out of his coat and fell to the ground. As he looked up, Nicholas was swept away in the arms of the devil. Andrew tried desperately to hold on to his brother's hand, but he just

couldn't. He could see his brother's face vanish in the clouded sky as he was carried away.

Their mother told Andrew not to search for Nicholas, ever. She could not risk losing another son. She warned him that he would most certainly die if he ever confronted the evil Sorcerer. Nicholas would surely be under some sort of spell, and this was nothing but danger. She made him swear to her that he would not attempt any such rescue. He swore to his mother, that he would not. This was the one promise he could not keep; it was too important to him.

Andrew kept searching the mountainsides as the two slowly made their way. The path began to narrow. The bare mountain began to fill with trees that eventually gave way to dense forest, and he now thought that they had entered the province of the evil Sorcerer.

Jenny seemed to be on high alert. She kept stopping and raising her nose in the air as if she had caught the scent of someone or something. He had never seen such alertness from her. He grabbed her around her neck and brought her close to himself. Are you ok, girl? Jenny licked his face but still looked as if she were sensing the presence of something. The two continued up the mountain. Then, Jenny took notice of a wolf moving alongside them on the ridge above the narrow road. She then caught the scent of a second wolf moving alongside them on the opposite ridge as well. Jenny was bigger than the two wolves combined, but they had a superior position to her. Andrew was unarmed other than the walking stick his father had given to him years ago, shortly before his death.

The boy's father was a great mountaineer. Several years ago, he had rescued a number of climbers who had been buried in an avalanche. He had rescued eight climbers and was headed back for the remaining climbers when a second avalanche, much bigger than the initial avalanche, slid down the mountain, killing him and the remaining two climbers.

Andrew's heart was broken over his father's death, and he vowed to find his brother for his mother, who was also devastated. However, time was becoming precious since their mother had a fever, and she could pass away any time now. Andrew was determined to find Nicholas for her at any cost or risk.

He was now seeing glimpses of the two wolves as they slowly became more conspicuous. It was now snowing harder and growing dark quickly.

As they turned the corner, they met a Great Black Wolf head-on, and Andrew stopped in his tracks. Jenny walked on. Despite how large she was, she was dwarfed in comparison to the enormity of this Great Black Wolf. Now Jenny stopped directly in front of the Great Black Wolf. They stood nose to nose. The two smaller wolves remained on the opposite ridges above the path. The odds were not in Jenny and Andrew's favor.

Andrew stood behind Jenny for several moments as the two great animals squared off. He thought he could see fire in the Great Black Wolf's eyes. Neither Jenny nor the Great Black Wolf moved. The moment hung in time as the two massive creatures faced one another. The Great Black Wolf raised his head slightly into the air as one of the smaller wolves up on the ridge had begun to creep down toward Jenny. The Great Black Wolf quickly turned to meet his comrade with an authoritative growl. The smaller wolf immediately retreated back up the ridge. Jenny did not move; she only observed. The Great Black Wolf turned his attention back at Jenny. He knew that Jenny had fought many a foe in her day when she was with the musher, but none could have had the ferociousness of this Great Black Wolf. The two great creatures leaned toward one another, closing the gap between them to inches. The Great Black Wolf bore his fangs at Jenny.

"Karatah!"

# CHAPTER FOUR

# The Charnelgoul

From farther up the road, out of sight from Andrew, came the loud command. The Great Black Wolf froze; then it rang out again.

The fire was suddenly gone from the Great Black Wolf's eyes, and he turned and began walking up the path, which now narrowed even more. The two smaller wolves remained still. Jenny followed, and then Andrew proceeded up the path. The two smaller wolves brought up the rear.

They traveled for more than an hour until they reached a clearing in the dense forest. A large fire was burning. The Great Black Wolf walked over, turned, and sat down on one side of the raging fire. Andrew caught up to Jenny, and the two stood side by side. The two wolves to the rear took up positions on the perimeter of the clearing. The forest was quiet except for the crackling of the fire.

In the next moment, a large figure arose from behind the fire and stared at them. Once Andrew's eyes grew accustomed to the light of the fire, he began to focus on the figure behind the fire.

"I am the Charnelgoul. What right of passage have you to be in this province? You are trespassing on the Sorcerer's property," he declared.

He recognized the voice as the same one that had given the Karatah command to the Great Black Wolf, whose loyalty seemed solely to the Charnelgoul.

"My name is Andrew. I have been looking for you."

"Why?"

"I think we have something in common."

The Charnelgoul remained silent and walked around from the backside of the fire, standing only a few feet from Andrew and Jenny. Andrew could see the distortion of the Charnelgoul's face. His ears were slightly pointed, and he had sunken eyes with large eyebrows. He had the appearance of a gargoyle. However, he somehow felt that the man before him, in whatever form, was not inherently evil.

"I am the immortal protector of the Sorcerer, guardian of evil," bellowed the Charnelgoul.

"We have something in common. We both have a birthmark on the center of our backs in the shape of a star with eight radiant points of light." With that, Andrew removed his coat and shirt and showed the Charnelgoul his back. There, on his back, was a faint birthmark in the shape of a star with eight radiant points of light.

"That means nothing to me. I have no such mark," replied the Charnelgoul.

"How do you know? Have you looked?" questioned Andrew.

"This is nonsense," replied the Charnelgoul angrily. Andrew then removed a small mirror from inside his coat pocket and approached the Charnelgoul.

"No!" said the Charnelgoul as he struck a blow to Andrew's chest with his fist, making him fall backward to the ground.

Jenny started to engage, but the Great Black Wolf intercepted her, so she could not help Andrew.

Andrew got up. "No girl, stay. I know you, Charnelgoul."

The Charnelgoul then pushed Andrew to the ground with both hands, applying greater force this time.

"You can hit me all you want. You can even kill me. I will not strike you, no matter what you do to me," he shouted in pain as he staggered to his feet.

The Charnelgoul pulled his fist back and was about to hit Andrew again when he paused and looked closely at his face. His eyes closed for a moment as his mind transgressed back to his short-lived childhood. He remembered when the Prince of Darkness had whisked him away many years ago. As he was being swept away by the arms of the devil, his little brother tried desperately to hold on to his hand but just couldn't. He could see his little brother's face vanish in the dust as he was carried away. Now, so many years later, that same boy had returned.

Andrew said, "Please, just trust me," and he put his hand lightly on the Charnelgoul's chest. The Charnelgoul grabbed his hand and held it. The two were face to face, Andrew barely able to stand. The Charnelgoul then turned around and pulled up his coat, vest, and shirt beneath. The Charnelgoul's back showed scars from old battle wounds. Andrew got his breath back and looked at the Charnelgoul's back. At first, Andrew could not see any remnants of the star birthmark. He moved closer and turned the Charnelgoul slightly toward the fire to get more light. In a moment, it appeared. Faint, but it was there, a star with eight radiant points of light.

"See, look for yourself," he said as he held a mirror for the Charnelgoul to see the mark over his shoulder. He stared for a long time before turning his head, pulling down his shirt, vest, and coat, and slowly walking to the other side of the fire.

"You are my brother, Nicholas," Andrew proclaimed.

There was a long silence between them. Nicholas was very confused. Suddenly, the spell that had fogged his mind and memories for so long, disappeared. He could now remember his brother. The years of faint memories now returned to the light.

"Andrew, my brother?"

"Yes, I knew it." He hugged Nicholas, and, at first, Nicholas didn't know what to do, but then wrapped his arms around Andrew.

"I cannot leave this place because of the Sorcerer. He will kill me and you if he finds out we are brothers. I can't risk your life."

"I have come to bring you back to our mother. She is sick and wants to see her son once more before she passes. Let's go to the castle and break whatever bonds hold you here," demanded Andrew.

Nicholas stared at Andrew for a long time. Then he turned and said, "You will have to wait just outside the castle, out of sight of the Sorcerer. I will then confront the Sorcerer myself. I will have to tell him that I have to travel down the mountain in search of invaders that I suspect have entered his territory. I will maybe have one day's leave at the most."

Andrew had no choice but to follow his brother's instruction. "Ok, my brother."

"This way then." They were off to the castle. It took

them more than an hour to ascend to the top of the mountain to the castle next to the Great Tree.

They reached a hidden spot out of the direct sight of the castle. It was a small hut under the cover of the Great Tree that Nicholas used on occasion to keep close watch on the province.

"Wait here until I get back. If I do not return, leave this province, and never return again, ever."

"I understand."

While Nicholas was gone, Andrew had a feeling that he was being watched or sensed the presence of someone nearby. Jenny was alert as well. He associated it with just being nervous.

Nicholas returned and explained that the Sorcerer had granted his request to travel down the mountain in search of potential invaders.

"Excellent!" Andrew was excited. He then went on to explain to Nicholas where their mother was living, but said that it would be at least a month's journey to get there. Nicholas told his brother to hush, as he could travel that distance and be back by sunset tomorrow.

"But how?" questioned Andrew.

"The magic carriage and reindeer can travel the distance and return in time," explained Nicholas. "Now get some rest and do not stray from here while I'm gone. Good night, brother."

"Good night," replied Andrew as he watched his brother leave.

As Nicholas prepared for his long journey, Andrew lay awake gazing out from under the Great Tree. He could see the village below and the castle against the moonlight. He thought he was in some type of a dream, but the weariness from his extended travels and the excitement of the day finally overcame him and he fell asleep with Jenny at his feet as always.

# CHAPTER FIVE

# The Return

Andrew awoke the next morning to the sound of a carriage being hitched. He looked out from under the Great Tree and could see Nicholas and the Great Black Wolf below. Nicholas was hitching a reindeer to the carriage. Within a few minutes, they were gone. Although he was cold and a bit uncomfortable, nothing could dampen the thought of Nicholas arriving to see their mother. Andrew would have fulfilled his vow to their mother if Nicholas could make it in time. That feeling of another presence was still there, but he just shook his head.

Nicholas arrived late in the morning to the town. He stowed the carriage on the outskirts of the town and told the Great Black Wolf to stay and protect the carriage while he was gone. He walked the rest of the way into town. He found the small brownstone building rather quickly. He stood in the front of the building, draped in his large cape, with a hood covering his face. He walked up the steps, entered the building's outer door, and knocked on the inner door. A young woman answered the door. Nicholas announced himself, saying that he was there to see his mother. Maggie was a young girl of 16 who was taking care of Nicholas' mother. When she caught sight of Nicholas, she gasped for a moment and then fainted. Nicholas quickly entered and caught Maggie before she hit the ground and laid her on a bed nearby. He did not want to scare his mother, as he knew his appearance was menacing. He kept his face covered with his cape, so as not to scare his mother. He heard his mother's voice coming from the bedroom, trying to discern what all the commotion was about. He descended the hallway to his mother's room to see her for the first time in more than a decade/

She was lying in the bed with her head propped up by many pillows. Her eyes were closed as he approached. He stood by her for a moment before she slowly opened her eyes. She was weak from the fever. She extended her hand to him. He grasped it gently with both hands.

She said, "Nicholas, is that you, my son?"

"Yes, mother, it is me, Nicholas."

"Thank goodness you are alright."

He dropped to one knee and kissed her hand and then held it against his cheek as he said, "It is me, mother, your faithful son." She squeezed his hands as hard as she could.

A moment later, Maggie entered the room and gasped again. "It's all right, Maggie. It's my son, Nicholas. Please get us some tea if you would."

"Yes, madam," Maggie said and left the room.

His mother's eyesight was almost gone. She could not make out any of his facial features and thus, she was spared the nature of her son's deformities. Nicholas and his mother spent the entire afternoon together just enjoying each other's presence. It had been so long.

Now it was nearing sundown, and Nicholas knew he had to return to the castle. He put his hands on each side of his mother's face and kissed her on the forehead.

"I must go, mother," he said. "Andrew will be home soon, I promise you. I love you with all my heart."

"I thank you, my son, but I will pass before I see either of you again, that I know for certain," she responded with a soft smile and continued, "I have always loved you, and I knew you would return one day. I missed you terribly." She squeezed his hand and asked him to come close to her. She said, "Listen to me carefully, Nicholas." She whispered into his ear in a very faint voice.

He was speechless after what he had just learned from his mother. He felt a great responsibility and at the same time, a deep sense of sorrow for his part in being the protector of the evil Sorcerer's kingdom. He had not done enough to stop the Sorcerer's hunt for the children who wandered into his kingdom and those delivered by the Prince of Darkness. Although he had scared many a child away, still some made it through and were devoured by the evil Sorcerer's powers. It was impossible for him to stop. Now it was time to put an end to it all. He sensed that the farther he was from the Sorcerer, the weaker his hold was upon Nicholas and his thoughts.

"Go now, Godspeed," his mother interrupted his thoughts.

He kissed his mother one last time, knowing that she would soon die and he would never see her again. He had no more time; Andrew and the Sorcerer were waiting.

"Now I must go, mother." He quickly left the room.

"Goodbye, Maggie. Thank you for your hospitality."

Maggie waved as he hurried to the front door and said, "Goodbye, Nicholas."

He hurried through the streets to the outskirts of the town where the carriage was stowed. He hitched the reindeer to the carriage, and off he went on his return trip to the castle. He only had a few hours until sunset.

# CHAPTER SIX

# The Sorcerer

Andrew spent most of the day under the protection of the Great Tree as Nicholas had told him to, but it was nearing sunset and he became very anxious. As he was looking toward the castle, he saw two kids being dragged into the castle by a group of goblins. He decided he could not let any more children get hurt, so he and Jenny headed up to the castle.

He found his way to a great hall. It was empty, and he stood in the middle of the great hall, all alone except for Jenny. The walls ascended into the deep darkness above and seemed to vanish. Then Andrew felt another presence in the room. Jenny began to growl.

It was the Sorcerer, who appeared from the darkness accompanied by a small army of goblin-like creatures. The Sorcerer's awesome presence was overwhelming. The goblins were frightening miniatures of evil, with pointed heads, noses,

and ears. They had disproportionately large hands in comparison to their small bodies, finished with long, curled fingernails.

"Who are you, and how dare you enter my castle without permission?" proclaimed the Sorcerer.

Andrew remained silent.

"You look very familiar to me."

"Andrew, help us." It was Madeline and Michael. The evil Sorcerer had captured them. Just then, Andrew's heart dropped, and he felt a rush of fear go through his body. They must have secretly followed Andrew and Jenny up to the castle.

"Let them go!" he yelled.

"In good time, perhaps," replied the Sorcerer, and calmly continued, "Is your name Andrew?"

"Yes."

"It is my lucky day indeed." All the goblins laughed at the Sorcerer's words. The echo of the laughter made a deafening noise through the great hall. The Sorcerer continued, "I had you, but you slithered away just as I snatched you up. I always had the feeling you would come for your brother eventually. I'm really very sorry it has to end this way."

Andrew was puzzled trying to decipher what the Sorcerer meant. Then the Sorcerer realized his puzzlement.

"You don't know, do you?" the Sorcerer then laughed in triumph at his discovery that Andrew was totally unaware of his circumstance.

Andrew was pained by his inability to determine what the Sorcerer knew that he didn't. He and Jenny were now surrounded by the goblins.

Michael and Madeline cried out for Andrew, as tears streamed down both their faces. He now suspected that he possessed something or knew something that the Sorcerer wanted or feared, but what was it?

He felt that his life was in danger now, and he did not have the ability to defeat the monster that he faced. He felt a yearning to be at home, safe from the evil force that now confronted him. He did not want to die. He was scared.

# CHAPTER SEVEN

# The Conflict

Just as the sun was setting, Nicholas could see the outline of the Great Tree in the distance. He began to remember the nightmare he had been having since he was a young boy. It made him sad and angry, even without the knowledge of what was happening to Andrew inside the castle.

When he reached the castle, he parked the carriage and quickly entered the castle with the Great Black Wolf. He heard Andrew's voice in the great hall.

Nicholas entered the great hall, worried about what he was going to find.

"Oh, thank God you are here."

He said nothing, but Andrew could tell by his look that he was troubled.

Nicholas then turned his attention to the Sorcerer who was at the end of the hall. His small army of goblins surrounded him again.

"Your Lordship, I respectfully request that we allow this man and his young friends to go free."

"No!" the Sorcerer roared. "Now I have you both here in my kingdom. You and your brother must die per order of the Prince of Darkness."

Nicholas now knew that the Sorcerer knew that Andrew

was his brother and that they were in danger.

The Sorcerer removed his massive sword from the sheath at his side and swung it toward Andrew. Jenny sprang from her seated position and bit directly into the hand of the Sorcerer, causing him to pull the sword up short of striking Andrew. The Sorcerer yelled in a combination of pain and anger and flung Jenny across the room.

The Sorcerer then raised the sword once more, just as Nicholas stepped between Andrew and the Sorcerer, but this time, the Great Black Wolf sprung up and clamped her jaws around the Sorcerer's arm. The sword flew out of the Sorcerer's hand and landed at Nicholas' feet. The Sorcerer then threw the Great Black Wolf toward one of the pillars of the great hall. The Great Black Wolf pounded into a pillar and lay there limp.

A moment later, the Sorcerer approached the brothers. Nicholas said to Andrew, "Get your friends and go under the protection of the Great Tree." Just then, Nicholas confronted the Sorcerer who taunted him by saying, "You will obey me. You are my Charnelgoul."

Nicholas could feel the power of the Sorcerer pulling at his will. The Sorcerer was physically larger and much more menacing than Nicholas, and his will was all-consuming.

 Andrew went over to Jenny, "Come on, girl. Get up, please?" Jenny got herself up on her feet. "Follow me, girl." They made their way to

where a couple of ugly goblins were holding
Madeline and Michael. Andrew kicked each of the
goblins into a column, stunning them temporarily.
He grabbed the kids by the hand. They all raced
across the great hall, past the Sorcerer and Nicholas, and went out toward the protection of the
Great Tree.

"You are powerless in front of me. I created you," bellowed the Sorcerer as Nicholas raised his fist toward the
Sorcerer. Nicholas felt the Sorcerer trying to overpower him
with his will. He knew that the Sorcerer garnered much of his
power from the castle itself. Nicholas needed to lure the Sorcerer away from it.

Nicholas had an idea. He quickly grabbed the Sorcer-
er's sword at his feet. Then he raced toward the Great Black
Wolf slumped by a column and slid next to him, yelling,
"Come on, get up, my great black beast!"

The Sorcerer began to move toward Nicholas and the
Great Black Wolf as he ordered his goblins to converge on
Nicholas. The Great Black Wolf rose up, and Nicholas jumped
on his back and bolted toward the door, outrunning the goblins,
much to the astonishment of the evil Sorcerer.

Nicholas, on the back of the Great Black Wolf, gal-
loped toward the Great Tree. The Sorcerer and his goblins were
now in pursuit.

Nicholas and the Great Black Wolf arrived at the Great
Tree. Andrew was there with Madeline and Michael.

"Hide the kids in the tree," Nicholas told Andrew.

Andrew did as he was told.

His mother's words came into Nicholas' mind, "Son, remember the eight radiant points of star as depicted on your and Andrew's back? I know through my dreams that it is your answer to breaking away from the evil Sorcerer. He is not your father any longer but a personification of evil. You need to destroy him, or he will kill you and your brother. Don't doubt me, son."

The Sorcerer was now at the Great Tree and confronting Nicholas. Nicholas raised the Sorcerer's sword and pointed it toward him. The Sorcerer just laughed at him. He began to try to overpower Nicholas' will with his own superior powers, but out in the open, the Sorcerer had lost the power of the castle that fueled him.

Nicholas fought the will forced upon him by the Sorcerer. He closed his eyes and crisscrossed the Sorcerer with four quick strokes of the sword, forming an eight-point star on the Sorcerer's chest. Nicholas then flung the sword headlong into the center of the star, just as the Sorcerer yelled, "No!"

The instant the sword struck the center of the star, a bright flash of light burst from the insertion point and illuminated the entire mountainside with blinding intensity.

A moment later, the great light engulfed the Sorcerer.

For a brief moment, both Andrew and Nicholas could see the persona of their father returning to that of a normal man, as he was before. He mouthed his final words, "I am sorry, my sons," and then dropped to the ground lifeless.

In his place sprung up an evil spirit. The Prince of Darkness appeared from within the Sorcerer like a devilish soul, like nothing either of them had ever seen. Then the light brightened even further and clearly showed eight radiant points of light. The light blinded them all. Andrew got up and grabbed Nicholas by the arm. Together, they pushed the Prince of Darkness into the light and heard a loud, deafening scream of agony from him. The light began to be sucked back through the center point of its origin. Within the light, the Prince of Darkness was also pulled through the center point with a burst of energy so powerful that it shook the ground around them. Suddenly, he was gone and it was silent.

Nicholas and Andrew got up and realized that both the Sorcerer and the Prince of Darkness were gone and destroyed forever. Their father's body now lay there next to the sword, at the spot of the Prince of Darkness's final departure. Andrew looked at Nicholas and his face had softened. His grotesque gargoyle-like features were gone from his face.

A swarm of little elves suddenly surrounded Andrew and Nicholas. Andrew looked at Nicholas and asked, "Are these the missing children?"

Nicholas nodded yes.

The children had transformed from ugly goblins, created by the Prince of Darkness, into cute little elves. In the midst of the elves were Michael and Madeline, who came rushing up to Andrew and hugged him tight. They were all right.

Jenny got up from under the Great Tree, walked over to the Great Black Wolf, and began licking his face. The Great Black Wolf's eyes were open wide, and there was no hint of the fiery red gaze.

Nicholas then took Andrew by the arm. He told Andrew what their mother had told him: the Sorcerer was their real father. He and a small band of brave men had tried to hunt down and kill the Prince of Darkness, but he was too strong. The Prince of Darkness had killed them all except their father, whom he kidnapped and corrupted through his evil ways and magical spells into an evil Sorcerer. They were both very young when this happened.

Andrew paused for a time, digesting what he had just learned. Then he shook his head and told Nicholas, "Our fathers—both of them, the fathers we knew—loved us in different ways. Both died heroes on mountainsides. The evil that haunted our real father is now dead and will be forgotten forever."

Jenny and the Great Black Wolf went outside and began to howl madly toward the moon-filled night sky.

The crowd of elves, Nicholas, Andrew, Madeline, and Michael enjoyed the serenade from the shadow of the Great Tree. The howling was heard all the way to the remote village below.

Only two men in the world possessed the power to strike down the Prince of Darkness, and it was only through their unification that their strength became powerful enough to slay him and save their own father's soul from damnation.

# CHAPTER EIGHT

# The Celebration

It was Christmas Eve. Nicholas told Andrew to take Madeline, Michael, Jenny, and the Great Black Wolf back to the village. There, they were to gather up all the children and the townsfolk and lead them up to the Great Tree the next day, which was Christmas. Andrew did not ask any questions and set off to the village. It was a difficult trip, but they were led by the Great Black Wolf and Jenny.

As the party entered the village, they were met by Aurora and a crowd of searchers that were looking for Madeline and Michael. They froze in their footsteps with fear when they saw the Great Black Wolf approaching.

"It's okay!" yelled Andrew. "He won't hurt you; I promise."

"Sis!" yelled Michael. Aurora's fear disappeared and turned to joy as she saw Michael and Madeline were safe.

"Oh, thank goodness you are alright," she cried as she smothered them with kisses and hugs. She looked at Andrew and mouthed the words "thank you," as she was overwhelmed with joy and relief.

That night, Andrew explained to the townspeople his adventure at the castle, the destruction of the evil Sorcerer, the transformation of his brother Nicholas, and the plight of the children. They all agreed to gather the next day to begin the ascent to the Great Tree.

Andrew returned to the inn where he was greeted with a grateful smile from Aurora, who welcomed him back. That night, Andrew occupied the same room he had the first night he had arrived in the tiny village. He thought how things had changed in such a brief period of time. He looked around the room and saw Jenny and the Great Black Wolf snuggled together next to the glow of the fireplace. Andrew looked up to the castle and the Great Tree, both of which were illuminated by the moonlight in the crystal-clear sky. He wondered what Nicholas was doing that night. He missed him already. Then Andrew fell off to sleep.

When Andrew awoke, it was still dark outside, and it was beginning to snow again. He noticed a light in the distance. He looked closer and could see that the Great Tree was lit up with what appeared to be hundreds of candles, like a beacon in the night sky. Nicholas had been busy indeed, he thought.

The townsfolks and their children gathered the next day at the town square, and there was great excitement in the air on that beautiful Christmas day. Andrew was prepared to lead the townsfolk up to the Great Tree. As they left, Aurora, Michael, and Madeline walked with Andrew, with Jenny and the Great Black Wolf leading the way. As the crusade drew closer and closer to the Great Tree, its size, spectacular adornments, and lights became more marvelous.

The top of the Great Tree was crowned with a star with eight radiant points of light shining brightly. When they finally reached the Great Tree, they found its base covered with beautifully wrapped presents for all the townsfolk and their children. Everyone was in awe of the magical sight. Each man, woman, and child had gifts specially selected for them. The gifts were spectacular jewels of gold and silver, and wonderful toys of all sorts for the children.

Andrew went into the castle, but Nicholas was gone. There was an envelope inscribed with Andrew's name. He opened the letter and it read:

> *My dear brother,*
> *Thank you for rescuing me and allow-*
> *ing me to see mother one more time.*
> *She has passed on now, brother, but*
> *do not fear for she is at peace. I have*
> *many tasks to do, but I want you to*
> *occupy this castle. I shall visit you*
> *each year on Christmas.*
> *Be well my brother.*
> *Nicholas*

Andrew returned to his mother's home, and as Nicholas had foretold, she had passed the same Christmas day as the birth of the Great Tree celebration.

Each year, Nicholas returned to the castle as he had promised to bring gifts for all the children of the village. Andrew decorated the Great Tree every year for Christmas.

One year, Maggie left with Nicholas, and they were wed.

Andrew ended up marrying Aurora. They had a son whom they named Nicholas after his uncle.

The news of the Great Tree and the adventures that had

taken place there spread throughout the land, and a tradition of celebration was born. You see, there were no Christmas trees in the village because there had been no such traditions before then.

Soon, everyone's home was adorned with a Christmas tree, decorated in the tradition of the Great Tree, and in anticipation of the birth of baby Jesus. As for Nicholas, in acknowledgement of his efforts in the celebration of Christmas, the Great Church bestowed sainthood upon him, which made him Saint Nicholas. He arrived each Christmas Eve, leaving gifts for all the children of the world in celebration of Christmas. He became so popular and beloved over the years that he became known as Santa Claus, the great saint. Each Christmas tree had the same symbolic crown: a star with eight radiant points of light.

Nicholas returned to the castle one Christmas Eve and met with Andrew. Nicholas' small carriage and one reindeer had grown to twelve reindeer and a huge sleigh. The elves were still with Nicholas. It was Nicholas' past that continued to haunt him. He decided, perhaps as a self-punishment for his past deeds as the Charnelgoul, to move to a very isolated part of the northernmost part of the territory with his wife and the elves, where they lived in solitude, but also in peace.

The Prince of Darkness was never seen thereafter.

Each Christmas Eve, however, Andrew and Saint Nicholas, along with Jenny and the Great Black Wolf, visited the memorial of their mother and prayed to her, thanking her for bringing them back together.

Andrew was unsure of his fate, but he felt that Nicholas had been blessed with immortality, which made Andrew secure in the knowledge that Nicholas would always bring hope and happiness to the world.

Andrew, Aurora, and young Nicholas, along with Jenny and the Great Black Wolf and many of their furry friends, would watch each Christmas Eve as Saint Nicholas and his elves flew away in their magical sleigh filled with gifts for all the children of the world, shouting to all the townsfolk and children, as only Santa Claus could:

**"Merry Christmas to all and to all a good night."**

*The End*

## About The Author

A ble Barrett is former Los Angeles County Deputy District Attorney and U.S. Department of Justice Organized Crime Strike Force Prosecutor. He is an avid animal lover and dedicated to the ethical treatment of all animals. He is manager of The Last Road Dog Animal Sanctuary in its efforts to rescue dogs, cats, and horses.

The Last Road Dog is an IRS Approved 501 (c)(3) Animal Public Welfare Charity.

For more information go to: www.thelastroaddog.com